Nibble Nibble

Paintings by

WENDELL MINOR

Nibble Nibble

These poems were first published within the collection *Nibble Nibble: Poems for Children*
by Margaret Wise Brown, © 1959.

 For information address HarperCollins Children's Books, a division of HarperCollins Publishers, 1350 Avenue of the Americas, New York, NY 10019.
www.harpercollinschildrens.com

Library of Congress Cataloging-in-Publication Data is available.
ISBN-10: 0-06-059208-7 (trade bdg.) — ISBN-13: 978-0-06-059208-0 (trade bdg.)
ISBN-10: 0-06-059209-5 (lib. bdg.) — ISBN-13: 978-0-06-059209-7 (lib. bdg.)

Typography by Carla Weise
1 2 3 4 5 6 7 8 9 10
❖
First Edition

To the timeless genius of
Margaret Wise Brown
— W.M.

Contents

Song of the Bunnies

Bunnies zip

And bunnies zoom

Bunnies sometimes sleep till noon

Zoom

Zoom

Zoom

Zoom

All through the afternoon

Zoom Zoom Zoom

This is the song of the bunnies.

Bunnies jump
And bunnies run
Bunnies also sit in the sun
This is the song of the bunnies.

Nibble Nibble Nibble

Nibble Nibble Nibble
Goes the mouse in my heart
Nibble Nibble Nibble
Goes the mouse in my heart
Nibble Nibble Nibble
Goes the mouse in my heart
And the mouse in my heart is
You.

Lippity Lippity Clip
Goes the rabbit in my heart
Lippity Lippity Clip
Goes the rabbit in my heart
Lippity Lippity Clip
Goes the rabbit in my heart
And the rabbit in my heart is
You.

Flippity Flippity Flop
Goes the fish in my heart
Flippity Flippity Flop
Goes the fish in my heart
Flippity Flippity Flop
Goes the fish in my heart
And the fish in my heart is
You.

Biff Bang Bang
Goes the hammer in my heart
Biff Bang Bang
Goes the hammer in my heart
Biff Bang Bang
Goes the hammer in my heart
And the hammer in my heart is
You.

Drum Drum Drum
Goes the drum in my heart
Drum Drum Drum
Goes the drum in my heart
Drum Drum Drum
Goes the drum in my heart
And the drum in my heart is
You.

Softly now beats the beat of my heart
Softly now beats the beat of my heart
Softly now beats the beat of my heart
All for the love of you.

The Rabbit Skip

Hop Skip Jump
A rabbit won't fight.

Hop Skip Jump
A rabbit won't bite.

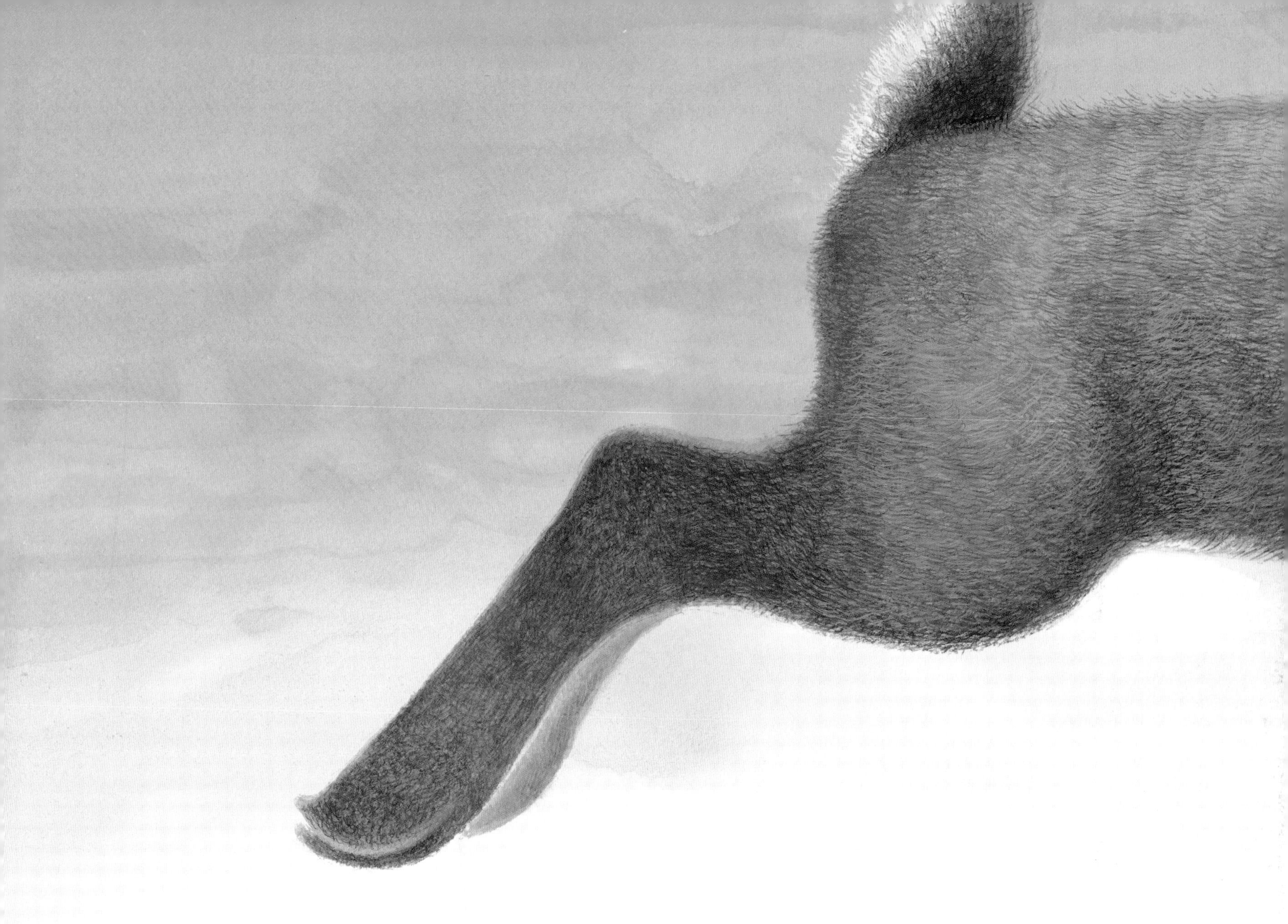

Hop Skip Jump
A rabbit runs light.

Hop Skip Jump
He's out of sight.

Song of Summer

Here comes a bunny
The first to stray
Out of April
And into May.

And here comes a robin
The first to fly
Out of June
And into July.

Here are the fireflies
Last to remember
The end of August
And first of September.

And here comes a caterpillar
The last to creep
Out of summer
And into sleep.

Cadence

There is music I have heard
Sharper than the song of bird
Sweeter still while still unheard
There beyond the inner ear.
Softer than the sounds I hear
Softer than the ocean's swell
In the caverns of a shell,

Tinier than cutting wings
Of flying birds and little things,
Like a cat's paw in the night
Or a rabbit's frozen fright.
This is the music I have heard
In the cadence of the word
Not spoken yet
And not yet heard.